"*If you want your children to be intelligent, read them fairy tales.*
If you want them to be more intelligent, read them more fairy tales."

– Albert Einstein

To our mother, who wanted us all to be intelligent.

FAMILY TREASURY OF CLASSIC TALES

ENCHANTED

EAST OF THE SUN AND WEST OF THE MOON

◆

IVAN AND THE CHESTNUT HORSE

◆

URASHIMA TARO

DESIGNED BY
JONAS BELL

EAST OF THE SUN AND WEST OF THE MOON

A NORWEGIAN FAIRY TALE

Once upon a time there was a poor husbandman who had many children and little to give them in the way of either food or clothing. They were all pretty, but the prettiest of all was the youngest daughter, who as she grew to a young woman became so beautiful that there were no bounds to her beauty.

So once, late on a Thursday evening when the weather was dark and wild and the rain was blowing so heavily that the walls of the cottage shook, they were all sitting together by the fireside. Each of them busy with something or other, when suddenly someone rapped three times against the window pane. The man went out to see what could be the matter, and when he got out there stood a great big white bear.

"Good-evening to you," said the White Bear.

"Good-evening," said the man.

"Will you give me the beautiful woman who is your youngest daughter?" asked the White Bear; "If you will, you shall be as rich as you are now poor."

Truly the man would have had no objection to be rich, but he thought to himself: "I must first ask my daughter about this," so he went in and told them that there was a great white bear outside who had faithfully promised to make them all rich if he might but have the youngest daughter. Looking at his daughter, the man said "You must decide this for yourself."

The young woman was generous of spirit and knowing she could help her family made up her mind to go. While the White bear waited patiently she washed and mended all her rags, made herself as smart as she could, and set out.

She seated herself on his back with her bundle, and thus they departed.

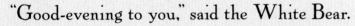

When they had gone a great part of the way, the White Bear said: "Are you afraid?"

"No, that I am not," said she.

"Keep tight hold of my fur, and then there is no danger," said he.

And thus she rode far, far away, until they came to a great mountain. Then the White Bear knocked on it, and a door opened, and they went into a castle where

there were many brilliantly lighted rooms which shone with gold and silver, likewise a large hall in which there was a well-spread table, and it was so magnificent that it would be hard to make anyone understand how splendid it was. The White Bear gave her a silver bell, and told her that when she needed anything she had but to ring this bell, and what she wanted would appear. So after she had eaten, and night was drawing near, she grew sleepy, and thought she would like to go to bed. She rang the bell, and scarcely had she touched it before she found herself in a chamber where a bed stood ready made for her, which was as pretty as anyone could wish to sleep in. But when she had lain down and put out the light a man came and lay down beside her, and behold it was the White Bear, who cast off the form of a beast during the night. This continued every night but she never saw him, for he always came after she had put out her light, and went away before daylight appeared.

So all went well and happily for a time, but then she began to be very sad and sorrowful, for all day long she had to go about alone; and she did so wish to go home to her father and mother and brothers and sisters. When the White Bear asked what it was that she wanted, she told him that in her parents' house at home there were all her brothers and sisters, and it was because she could not go to them that she was so sorrowful.

"There might be a cure for that," said the White Bear, "if you would grant me one promise. Your mother will wish to take hold of your hand, and will want to lead you into a room to talk with you alone; but that you must by no means do, or you will bring great misery on both of us." This the young girl promised, as she thought it would be easy to do.

And so one Sunday the White Bear came and said that they could now set out to see her father and mother. They went a long, long way, and it took a long, long time; but at last they came to a large white farmhouse, and it was so pretty that it was a pleasure to look at it.

"Your parents dwell here now," said the White Bear; "But do not forget what I said to you, or you will do much harm both to yourself and me."

"No, indeed," said she, "I shall never forget;" and as soon as she was at home the White Bear turned round and went back again.

There were such rejoicings when she went in to her parents house that it seemed as if they would never come to an end. Everyone thought that they could never be sufficiently grateful to her for all she had done for them. But in the afternoon, after they had dined at midday, all happened just as the White Bear had said. Her mother wanted to talk with her alone in her own chamber. But she remembered what the White Bear had said, and would not go.

"What we have to say can be said at any time," she answered.

But somehow or other her mother at last persuaded her, and she was forced to tell the whole story. So she told how every night a man came and lay down beside her when the lights were all put out, and how she never saw him, because he always went away before it grew light in the morning, and how she continually went about in sadness, thinking how happy she would be if she could but see him.

"I will teach you a way to see him," soothed her mother, "You shall have a bit of one of my candles, which you can take away with you, hidden in your breast. Look at him with that when he is asleep, but take care not to let any wax drop upon him."

So she took the candle, and hid it in her breast, and when evening drew near the White Bear came to fetch her away.

When she had reached home and had gone to bed it was just the same as it had been before, and a man came and lay down beside her, and late at night, when she could hear that he was sleeping, she got up, lit her candle, and let her light shine on him, and saw him, and he was the handsomest prince that eyes had ever beheld, and she loved him so much that it seemed to her that she must die if she did not kiss him that very moment. So she did kiss him; but while she was doing it she let three drops of hot wax fall upon his shirt, and he awoke.

"What have you done now?" said he; "You have brought misery on both of us. If you had but held out for the space of one year I should have been free. I have a stepmother who has bewitched me so that I am a white bear by day and a man by night; but now all is at an end between you and me, and I must leave you, and go to her. She lives in a castle which lies east of the sun and west of the moon, and there too is a princess with a nose which is three ells long, and she now is the one whom I must marry."

She wept and lamented, but all in vain, for go he must. Then she asked him if she could not go with him. But no, that could not be. "Can you tell me the way then, and I will seek you? That I may surely be allowed to do!"

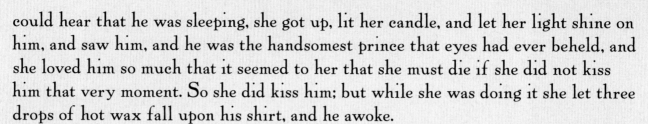

"Yes, you may try," said he; "but it lies east of
the sun and west of the moon, and never would
you find your way there."

When she awoke in the morning both the Prince and the castle were gone, and she was lying on a small green patch in the midst of a dark, thick wood. By her side lay the self-same bundle of rags which she had brought with her from her own home. So when she had rubbed the sleep out of her eyes, and wept till she was weary, she set out on her way, and thus she walked for many and many a long day, until at last she came to a great mountain. Outside it an aged woman was sitting, playing with a golden apple. The girl asked her if she knew the way to the Prince who lived with his stepmother in the castle which lay east of the sun and west of the moon, and who was to marry a princess with a nose which was three ells long.

"How do you happen to know about him?" inquired the old woman; "Maybe you are she who ought to have had him."

"Yes, indeed, I am," she said.

"So it is you, then?" said the old woman; "I know nothing about him except he dwells in a castle which is east of the sun and west of the moon. You will be a long time in getting to it, if ever you get to it at all; but you shall have the loan of my horse, and then you can ride on it to an old woman who is a neighbor of mine: perhaps she can tell you about him. You may take the golden apple with you for it may be of help."

So the girl continued until she came to a cliff, where she met another old woman, this one with a golden comb. She asked her of the prince and the old woman told her she knew nothing but that the prince lived a long way off in a castle east of the sun and west of the moon. Then the old woman gave her the comb in case it should help the girl.

So the girl continued on a wearisome long way, and after a very long time she came to a great mountain, where a third aged woman was sitting, spinning at a golden spinning-wheel. Of this woman, too, she inquired if she knew the way to the Prince, and where to find the castle which lay east of the sun and west of the moon. But it was only the same thing once again.

"Maybe it was you who should have had the Prince," said the old woman.

"Yes, indeed, I should have been the one," said the girl.

But this old crone knew the way no better. It was east of the sun and west of the moon, she knew that, "And you will be a long time in getting to it, if ever you get to it at all," she said; "Ride to the East Wind, and ask him: perhaps he may know where the castle is and will blow you there." And then she gave her the golden spinning wheel, saying: "Perhaps you may find that you have a use for it."

The girl had to ride for a great many days, and for a long and wearisome time, before she got there; but at last she did arrive, and then she asked the East Wind if he could tell her the way to the Prince who dwelt east of the sun and west of the moon. The East Wind knew of the prince, but had never blown so far as east of the sun and west of the moon. So the East Wind put the girl on his back and blew her to his brother the West Wind. The West Wind could not carry the girl to the castle either for he could not blow so far as east of the sun and west of the moon, but instead had her climb on his back and blew her to his brother the South Wind. The South Wind knew of the prince and his castle, but could not blow so far as east of the sun and west of the moon. "I must blow you to my brother the North Wind, for he is the strongest of us all. Perhaps he can carry you to the castle east of the sun and west of the moon." And the girl climbed on the South Wind's back and they blew to the North Wind, which I think did not take very long at all.

When the girl arrived at the North Wind she told him her story and then she asked, "Can you help me?"

"Yes," said the North Wind, "I know where it is. I once blew an aspen leaf there, but I was so tired that for many days afterward I was not able to blow at all. However, if you really are anxious to go there, and are not afraid to go with me, I will take you on my back, and try to blow you there."

"Get there I must," said she; "And if there is any way of going I will; and I have no fear, no matter how fast you go."

"Very well then," said the North Wind, and puffed himself up, and made himself so big and so strong that it was frightful to see him, and away they went, high up through the air, as if they would not stop until they had reached the very end of the world. And thus they travelled on and on, and a long time went by, and then yet more time passed, and as they found themselves above the sea, the North Wind grew tired, and more tired, and at last so utterly weary that he was scarcely able to blow any longer, and he sank and sank, lower and lower, until at last he went so low that the waves dashed against the heels of the poor girl he was carrying.

"Are you afraid?" said the North Wind.

"I have no fear," said she; and it was true. But they were not very far from land, and there was just enough strength left in the North Wind to enable him to throw her on to the shore, immediately under the windows of a castle which lay east of the sun and west of the moon.

The next morning she sat down beneath the walls of the castle to play with the golden apple, and the first person she saw was the maiden with the long nose, who was to have the Prince.

"How much do you want for that gold apple of yours, girl?" said she, opening the window.

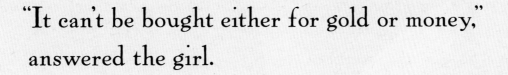

"It can't be bought either for gold or money," answered the girl.

"If it cannot be bought either for gold or money, what will buy it? You may say what you please," said the Princess.

"Well, if I may go to the Prince who is here, and be with him tonight, you shall have it," said the girl who had come with the North Wind.

"You may do that," said the Princess, for she had made up her mind what she would do.

So the Princess got the golden apple, but when the girl went up to the Prince's apartment that night he was asleep, for the Princess had so planned it. The Princess had given him a sleeping-drink of which he was unaware. The poor girl called to him, and shook him, and between whiles she wept; but she could not wake him. In the morning, as soon as day dawned, in came the Princess with the long nose, and drove her out of the room.

That day she sat down once more beneath the windows of the castle, this time using the golden comb. Again the Princess made a bargain with the girl. Again the girl could not wake the Prince, for the Princess had made sure he would sleep. Again the girl was driven from the room the next morning having been unable to speak to her Prince.

In the daytime she sat down once more beneath the windows of the castle, this time to spin with her golden spinning wheel, and the Princess with the long nose wanted to have that also. So she opened the window, and asked what she would take for it. The girl said what she had said each time previous, that it was not for sale, either for gold or for money, but if she could get leave to go to the Prince who lived there, and be with him during the night, she should have it.

"Yes," said the Princess, "I will gladly consent to that."

But in that place there were some folk who had been carried off, and they had been sitting in the chamber which was next to that of the Prince, and had heard how a woman had been in there who had wept and called on him the night before, and they told the Prince of this. So that evening, when the Princess came once more with her sleeping-drink, he pretended to drink, but threw it away behind him, for he suspected that it was a sleeping-drink. So, when the girl went into the Prince's room this time he was awake, and she had to tell him how she had come there.

"You have come just in time," said the Prince, "For I should have been married tomorrow; but I will not have the long-nosed Princess, and you alone can save me. I will say that I want to see what my bride can do, and bid her wash the shirt which has the three drops of wax on it. This she will consent to do, for she does not know that it is you who let them fall on it; and no one can wash them out but my one true love: it cannot be done by a pack of trolls; and then I will say that no one shall ever be my bride but the woman who can do this, and I know that you can."

There was great joy and gladness between them and the next day, when the wedding was to take place, the Prince said, "I must see what my bride can do."

"That you may do," said the stepmother.

"I have a fine shirt which I want to wear as my wedding shirt, but three drops of wax have got upon it which I want to have washed off, and I have vowed to marry no one but the woman who is able to do it. If she cannot do that, she is not worth having."

Well, that was a very small matter, they thought, and agreed to do it. The Princess with the long nose began to wash as well as she could, but, the more she washed and rubbed, the larger the spots grew.

"Ah! you can't wash at all," said the old troll-hag, who was her mother. "Give it to me."

But she too had not had the shirt very long in her hands before it looked worse still, and, the more she washed it and rubbed it, the larger and blacker grew the spots.

So the other trolls had to come and wash, but, the more they did, the blacker and uglier the shirt became, until at length it was as black as if it had been up the chimney.

"Oh," cried the Prince, "Not one of you is good for anything at all! There is a beggar-girl sitting outside the window, and I'll be bound that she can wash better than any of you! Come in, you girl there!" he cried.

So she came in.

"Can you wash this shirt clean?" he cried.

"Oh! I don't know," she said; "But I will try."

And no sooner had she taken the shirt and dipped it in the water than it was white as driven snow, and even whiter than that.

"I will marry you," said the Prince.

Then the old troll-hag flew into such a rage that she blew away, and the Princess with the long nose and all the little trolls must have chased after her, for they have never been heard of since.

The Prince and his bride set free all the folk who were imprisoned there, and took away with them all the gold and silver that they could carry, and moved far away from the castle which lay east of the sun and west of the moon.

The End

IVAN AND THE CHESTNUT HORSE

A RUSSIAN FAIRY TALE

I n a far away land where they pay people to keep its name a profound secret, there lived an old man who brought up his three sons just exactly in the way they should go. He taught them the three R's, and also showed them what books to read and how to read them. He was particularly careful about their education, for he had learned that to know things was to be able to do things.

At last, when he came to die, he gathered his three sons round his deathbed and cautioned them.

"Do not forget," he said, "do not forget to come and

read the prayers over my grave."

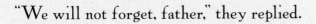

"We will not forget, father," they replied.

The two elder brothers were great big, strapping fellows, but the youngest one, Ivan, was a mere stripling. As they all stood around the bed of their dying father, he looked a mere reed compared to his proud, stout, elder brothers. But his eyes were full of fire and spirit, and the firm expression of his mouth showed great determination. When the father had breathed his last, and his two elder brothers wept without restraint, Ivan stood silent, his pale face set and his eyes full of the bright wonder of tears that would not melt.

On the day that they buried their father, Ivan returned to the grave in the evening to read prayers over it. He had done so, and was making his way homeward, when there was a great clatter of hoofs behind him; then, as he reached the village square, the horseman pulled up and dismounted quite near to him.

After blowing a loud blast on his silver trumpet, for he was the King's messenger, he cried in a loud voice:

"All and every man, woman and child, take notice, in the name of the King. It is the King's will that this proclamation be cried abroad in every town and village where his subjects dwell. The King's daughter, Princess Helena the Fair, has caused to be built for herself

a shrine having twelve pillars and twelve rows of beams. And she sits there upon a high throne till the time when the bridegroom of her choice rides by. And this is how she shall know him: with one leap of his steed he reaches the height of the tower, and, in passing, his lips press those of the Princess as she bends from her throne. Wherefore the King has ordered this to be proclaimed throughout the length and breadth of the land, for if any deems himself able so to reach the lips of the Princess and win her, let him try. In the name of the King I have said it!"

The blood of the youth of the nation, wherever this proclamation was issued, took flame and leapt to touch the lips of Princess Helena the Fair. All wondered to whose lot this lucky fate would fall. Some said it would be to the most daring, others contended that it was a matter of the leaping powers of the steed, and yet others that it depended not only on the steed but on the daring skill of the rider also.

When the three brothers had listened to the words of the King's messenger they looked at one another; at least the elder two did, for it was apparent to them that Ivan, the youngest, was quite out of the competition, whereas they, two splendid handsome fellows, were distinctly in it.

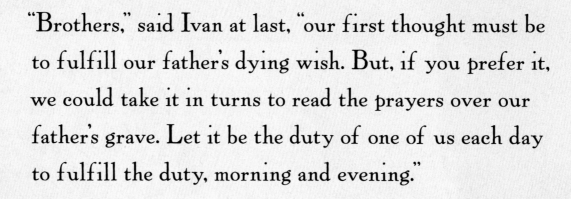

"Brothers," said Ivan at last, "our first thought must be to fulfill our father's dying wish. But, if you prefer it, we could take it in turns to read the prayers over our father's grave. Let it be the duty of one of us each day to fulfill the duty, morning and evening."

The elder brothers agreed readily to this, but, when Ivan asked whose turn it should be the next day, they both began to make excuses.

"As for me," said the eldest, "I must go and order the work of the farm my father left me, and that will take seven days."

"And for me," said the younger, "I must see to the estate which is my part of the inheritance, and that also will take seven days."

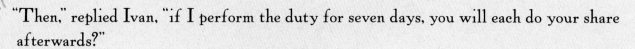

"Then," replied Ivan, "if I perform the duty for seven days, you will each do your share afterwards?"

His brothers agreed still more readily than before. Then they went their ways, Ivan full of thoughts of his father, and the other two to train their jumping horses, the one on his farm and the other on his estate. And both laughed to themselves, for neither knew the purpose of the other.

How they curled their hair and cleaned their teeth, and practiced "prunes and prisms" with their mouths close to the looking glass! — so that when, at one bound of their magnificent steeds, they reached the level of the Princess's lips, to aim the kiss that was to win the prize, they would make a brave show, and a conquering one. As for their little brother, they each thought he could go on praying over their father's grave as long as he liked,—it would be the best thing he could do, and it would not interfere with their secret plans, so carefully concealed from each other and from him.

At the end of the seven days the youngest brother summoned them to keep their agreement, and asked which of them would read the prayers, morning and evening, for the second seven days.

"I have done my part," he said; "now it is for you to arrange between you which one shall continue the sacred duty."

The two elder brothers looked at each other and then at Ivan.

"As for me," said one, "I care little who does it, so long as I am free to get on with my business, which is more important."

"And as for me," said the other, "I am in no mind to watch each blade of grass growing on the grave. I cannot really afford the time, I am so busy. You, Ivan,—you are different: you are not a man of affairs; how could you spend your time better than reading prayers over our father's grave?"

"So be it," replied Ivan. "You get back to your work and I will attend to the sacred duty for another seven days."

The two elder brothers went their separate ways, and for seven more days devoted their entire attention to training their horses for the flying leap at the Princess's lips.

The morning of the great day came. The eldest brother had chosen from his horses a magnificent black one with arched neck and flowing mane and tail. The second brother had selected a bay equally splendid. And now, at sunrise, they were, each unknown to the other, combing their well-curled hair, re-dyeing their moustaches, and booting and trapping themselves for the wonderful display of prowess the day was to bring forth. And they did not forget to make sure that their lips were as fit as they were anxious for the "high kiss."

At the appointed time they rode and drew their lots, and neither was altogether surprised at seeing his brother among the host of competitors for the hand of Helena the Fair. Their surprise came later, when Ivan arrived on the scene.

It so happened in this way: that, towards evening, when his two brothers had each had their last try to leap up to the Princess's lips and failed, like every one else, Ivan himself was reading the prayers over his father's grave. Suddenly a great emotion came over him, and he stopped in his reading. He was filled with a longing to look just for once upon the face of Helena the Fair, for whose favor he knew that the most splendid in the land were competing with their wonderful steeds. So strong was this longing that he broke down and, bending over his father's grave, wept bitterly.

And then a strange thing happened. His father heard him in his coffin, and shook himself free from the damp earth, and came out and stood before him.

"Do not weep, Ivan, my son," he said. And Ivan looked up and was terrified at the sight of him.

"Nay, my son, do not fear me," his father went on. 'You have fulfilled my dying wish, and I will help you in your trouble. You wish to look upon the face of Helena the Fair, and so it shall be.

> With this he drew himself up, and called in a loud
> voice. Ivan listened closely as nearer and nearer came a
> galloping sound, until at last, with a thundering snort
> and a ringing neigh, a beautiful chestnut horse appeared,
> circled round them, and then came to a halt before them,
> its eyes, ears, and nostrils shooting flames of fire.

Then came a voice, and Ivan knew it was the voice of the chestnut horse with the proudly arched neck and flowing mane:

"What is your will? Command me and I obey!"

The father took Ivan by the hand and led him to the horse's head.

"Enter here at the right ear," he said, "and pass through, and make your way out at the left ear. By so doing you will be able to command the horse, and he will do whatever you may wish that a horse should do."

So Ivan, doubting nothing, passed in at the right ear of the chestnut horse and came out at the left; and immediately there was a wonderful change in him. He was no longer a dreamy youth: he was at once a man of affairs, and the light of a high ambition shone in his eyes.

"Mount! Go, win the Princess Helena the Fair!" said his father, and he immediately vanished.

With one spring Ivan was astride the chestnut horse, and, in another moment, they were speeding like lightning towards the shrine of Helena the Fair.

The sun was setting, and the two elder brothers, disconsolate, were about to withdraw from the field, when, startled by the cries of the people, they saw a steed come galloping on, well ridden, and at a terrific pace. They turned to look and they marked how Helena the Fair, disappointed in all of the others, leaned out to watch the oncoming horseman. And the whole crowd turned and stood to await the possible event.

On came the chestnut horse, his nostrils snorting fire, his hoofs shaking the earth. He neared the shrine, and, to a masterful rein, rose at a flying leap. The daring rider looked up and the Princess leaned down, but he could not reach her lips, ready as they were.

The whole field now stood at gaze as the chestnut horse with its rider circled round and came up again. And this time, with a splendid leap, the brave steed bore its rider aloft so that the fragrant breath of the Princess seemed to meet his nostrils, and yet his lips did not meet hers.

Again they circled round while all stood still and tense. Again the chestnut steed rose to the leap, and, this time, the lips of Ivan met those of the Princess in a long sweet kiss, for the chestnut horse seemed to linger in the air at the top of its leap while that kiss endured.

Then, while the Princess looked on, horse and rider reached the ground and disappeared like lightning.

On the following day there was a great gathering at the palace, and, in the midst of it, sat Princess Helena the Fair demanding her bridegroom — the one who had leapt to her lips and won her from all others. Her heart and soul were his. The half of her kingdom to come was his. She, herself, was his; — where was he?

A search was made among the highest in the land, but, fearing a demand for the repetition of the leap and the kiss, none came forward. Ivan sat at the back, a humble spectator.

"She is thinking of that leap and that kiss," said he to himself. "When she sees me as I am, then let her judge."

But love, though blind, has eyes. The Princess rose from her seat and swept a glance over the people. She saw the two handsome elder brothers and passed them by as dirt. Then, by the light of love, she spied sitting in a corner, where the lights were low, the hero of the chestnut horse,— the one who had leapt high and reached her lips in the first sweet kiss of love.

She knew him at once, and, as all looked on in wonder, she made her way to that dim corner, took him by the hand without a word, and led him up, past the throne of honor, to an antechamber, where, with the joyous cries of the people ringing in their ears, their lips met a second time — at the summit of a leap of joy.

At that moment the King entered, knowing all.

"What is this?" he asked.

Then he smiled, for he understood his daughter, and knew that she had not only chosen her one true love, but had won her choice.

"My son," he added, without waiting for an answer, "you and yours will reign after me. Look to it! Now let us go to supper."

The End

URASHIMA TARO

A JAPANESE FAIRY TALE

A very long time ago there lived in Japan a young fisherman named Urashima Taro. His father before him had been a very expert fisherman, but Urashima's skill in the art so far exceeded that of his father, that his name as a fisher was known far and wide beyond his own little village. It was a common saying that he could catch more fish in a day than a dozen others could in a whole week.

But it was not only as a fisher that Urashima excelled. Wherever he was known, he was loved for his kindly heart. Never had he hurt even the meanest creature. Indeed, had it not been necessary to catch fish for his living, he would always have fished with a straight hook, so as to catch only such fish as wished to be caught.

One evening, as Urashima was returning from a hard day's fishing, he met a number of boys all shouting and laughing over something they were attacking in the middle of the road. It was a tortoise they had caught and were abusing. Between them all, what with sticks and stones and other kinds of torture, the poor creature seemed almost frightened to death.

Urashima could not bear to see a helpless thing treated in that way, so he interfered.

"Boys!" he said, "that's no way to treat a harmless dumb creature. You'll kill the poor thing!"

The young boys ran off laughing, on to their next game, leaving Urashima alone with the tortoise.

Urashima looked at the tortoise, which looked back at him with wistful eyes full of meaning; and, though it could not speak, the young fisherman understood it perfectly, and his tender heart went out to it.

"Poor little tortoise!" he said, holding it up and stroking it gently to soothe its fears, "you are all right with me. But remember, sweet little one, you've had a narrow squeak of losing a very long life. How long is it? Ten thousand years, they say. Now I'm going to take you right back to the sea, so that you can swim away to your home and to your own people. But promise me you will never let yourself be caught again."

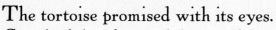

The tortoise promised with its eyes. So wistful and grateful were they, that Urashima felt he could never forget them.

By this time he was down on the seashore, and there he placed the tortoise in the sea and watched it swim away. Then he went home feeling very happy about the whole thing.

Morning was breaking when Urashima pushed off his boat for his day's fishing. The sea was calm, and the air was full of the soft, sweet warmth of summer. Soon he was out skimming over the blue depths, and when the tide began to ebb, he drifted far beyond the other fishermen's boats, until his own was lost to their sight.

It was such a lovely morning when the sun rose and slanted across the waters, that, when he thought of the short span of human life, he wished that he had thousands of years to live, like the tortoise he had rescued from the boys the day before.

As he was dreaming these thoughts, he was suddenly startled by a sweet voice calling his name. It fell on his ears like the note of a silver bell dropping from the skies. Again it came, nearer than before:

"Urashima! Urashima!"

He looked all around on the surface of the sea, thinking that some one had hailed him from a boat, but there was no one there, as far as the eye could reach.

And now he heard the voice again close at hand, and, looking over the side of the boat, he saw a tortoise looking up at him, and he knew by its eyes that it was the same tortoise he had restored to the sea the previous day.

"So we meet again," he said pleasantly. "Fancy you finding me in the middle of the ocean! What is it, you funny little tortoise? Do you want to be caught again, eh?"

"I have looked for you," replied the tortoise, "ever since dawn, and when I saw you in the boat I swam after you to thank you for saving my life."

"Well, that's very nice of you to say that. I haven't much to offer you, but if you would like to come up into the boat and dry your back in the sun we can have a chat."

The tortoise was pleased to accept the invitation, and Urashima helped it up over the side. Then, after talking of many things, the tortoise remarked, "I suppose you have never seen Rin Gin, the Dragon Sea-King's palace, have you?"

Urashima shook his head.

"No," he replied. "They tell me it is a beautiful sight, but in all the years that I have spent upon the sea I have never been invited to the Dragon King's palace. It's some distance from here, isn't it?"

"I do not think you believe there is such a place," replied the tortoise, who had seen a twinkle in Urashima's eye. "Yet I assure you it exists, but a long way off right down at the bottom of the sea. If you would really like to see Rin Gin, I will take you there."

"That is very kind of you," said Urashima with a polite bow, which pleased the tortoise greatly; "but I am only a man, you know, and cannot swim a long way under the sea like a tortoise."

But the little creature hastened to reassure him.

"That's not at all necessary," it said. "I'll do the swimming and you can ride on my back."

Urashima laughed. The idea of his riding on the back of a tortoise that he could hold in his hand was funny, and he said so.

"Never mind how funny it is," said the tortoise; "just get on and see." And then, as Urashima looked at it, the tortoise grew and grew and grew until its back was big enough for two men to ride upon.

"What an extraordinary thing!" exclaimed Urashima. "Right you are, friend tortoise, I'll come with you." And with that he jumped on.

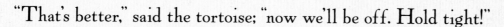

"That's better," said the tortoise; "now we'll be off. Hold tight!"

The next moment the tortoise plunged into the sea, and dived down and down until Urashima thought they would never be able to reach the surface again in a thousand years. At last he caught sight of a land below them, shining all green with the filtered sunlight. They passed over a vast green plain, at the further side of which, in a village at the foot of high mountains, shone the splendid portals of a magnificent palace.

"See!" said the tortoise, "that is the entrance to Rin Gin. We shall soon be there now. How do you feel?"

"Quite well, thank you!" And indeed, when Urashima felt his clothes he found they were quite dry, which was really not so surprising because, as he was borne swiftly through the water, there was a space of air around him all the time, so that not only was he kept quite dry, but he could breathe quite easily.

When they drew nearer to the great gate, Urashima could see beyond it, half hidden by the trees, the shining domes of the palace. It was indeed a magnificent

place, unlike anything ever seen in the lands above the sea.

Now they were at the great gate, and the tortoise stopped at the foot of a flight of coral steps and asked him to dismount.

"You can walk now, Urashima," and it led the way. Then the gatekeeper, a royal sturgeon, challenged them, but the tortoise explained that Urashima was a mortal from the great kingdom of Japan, who had come to visit the Sea King, and the gatekeeper immediately showed them in.

As they advanced, they were met by the courtiers and officials. The dolphin, the bonito, the great cuttle-fish, the bright-red bream; and the mullet, the sole, the flounder, and a host of other fishes came forward and bowed gracefully before the tortoise; indeed, such homage did they pay that Urashima wondered what sway the tortoise held in this kingdom beneath the sea. Then, when the visitor was introduced, they all cried out a welcome. And the dolphin, who was a high official, remarked, "We are delighted to see so distinguished a stranger from the great kingdom of Japan. Welcome to the palace of the Dragon King of the Sea!"

Then all the fishes went in a procession before them to the interior of the palace.

Now the humble fisherman had never been in such a magnificent place before. He had never learned how to behave in a royal palace but, though much amazed, he did not feel at all shy. As he followed his guides, he suddenly noticed that the tortoise had disappeared, but he soon forgot this when he saw a lovely Princess, surrounded by her maidens, come forward to greet him.

She was more beautiful than anything on earth, and her robes of pink and green changed color like the surface of the sea at sunset in some sheltered cove. There were threads of pure gold in her long hair, and, as she smiled, her teeth looked like little white pearls. She spoke soft words to him, and her voice was as the murmur of the sea.

Urashima was so enchanted that he could not speak a word; but he had heard that one must always bow low to a Princess, and he was about to do so when

the Princess tripped to his side, and, taking his hand in hers, led him off into a splendid apartment, where she conducted him to the place of honor and asked him to be seated.

"Listen to me, Urashima," she said in a low, sweet voice. "I am filled with joy at welcoming you to my father's palace, and I will tell you why. Yesterday you saved the precious life of a tortoise. Urashima, I was that tortoise! It was my life that you saved!"

Urashima could not believe this at first, but, when he gazed into her beautiful eyes, he remembered their wistful look, and her sweet words were spoken in the same voice as that which had called his name upon the sea. And he was so astonished that he could not speak.

"Would you like to live here always, Urashima,— to live in everlasting youth, never growing tired or weary? This is the land of eternal summer, where all is joy, and neither death nor sorrow may come. Stay, Urashima, and I, the Princess of my father's kingdom, will be your bride!"

Urashima felt it was all a dream; yet, if it were, then from the very heart of that dream he replied in words that came of their own accord.

"Sweet Princess, if I could thank you ten thousand times I should still want to thank you all over again. I will stay here; nay—more: I simply cannot go, for this is the most wonderful place I have ever dreamed of, and you are the most wonderful thing in it."

A smile spread over her lovely face. She bent towards him, and their lips met in the first sweet kiss of love.

Then, as if by this a magic button had been pressed, a wedding feast was prepared and the happy pair pledged themselves in marriage, while the music played and glad songs were sung.

The next day, the Princess showed Urashima over the palace, and pointed out all the wonders it contained. The whole place was fashioned out of pink and white coral, beautifully carved and inlaid everywhere with priceless pearls.

It was a wonderful country to live in and never grow old. No wonder that Urashima forgot his home in Japan, forgot his old parents, forgot even his own name. But, after three days of indescribable happiness, he seemed to wake up to a memory of who he was and what he had been. The thought of his poor old father and mother searching everywhere for him, perhaps mourning him as dead; the surroundings of his simple home, his friends in the little village,—all these things rushed in on his mind and turned all his joy to sadness.

"Alas!" he cried, "How can I stay here any longer? My mother will be weeping and wringing her hands, and my father bowing his old head in grief. I must go back this very day."

So, towards evening, he sought the Princess, his bride, and said sadly:

"Alas! alas! You have been so kind to me and I have been so very, very happy, that I have forgotten and neglected my parents for three whole days. They will think I am dead and will weep for me. I must say farewell and leave you."

Then the Princess wept and besought him to remain with her. "Beloved!" he protested, "in our land of Japan there is no crime so terrible as the crime of faithlessness to one's parents. I cannot face that, and you would not have me do it. Yet it will break my heart to leave you—break my heart—break my heart! I must go, beloved, but only for one day; then I will return to you."

"Alas!" cried the Princess, "What can we do? You must act as your heart guides you. I would give the whole world to keep you with me just one more day. But I know it cannot be. I know something of your land and your love of your parents. I will await your return: you will be gone only one day. It will be a long day for me, but, when it is over, and you have told your parents all, you will find a tortoise waiting for you by the seashore, and you will know that tortoise: it is the same that will take you back to your parents for one day! But wait, I have something to give you before you go."

The Princess left him hastily and soon returned with a golden casket, set with pearls and tied about with a green ribbon made from the floating seaweed. She gave it to him saying, "When you go up to the dry land you must always have this box with you, but you must never open it till you return to me."

"I promise, I promise. I will never open it till I return to you." Urashima went on his bended knee as he said these words.

"Farewell!"

"Farewell!"

Urashima was then conducted to the gate by the court officials, led by the dolphin. There the royal sturgeon blew a loud whistle, and presently a large tortoise came up. Urashima mounted on its back and down they went into the deep, green sea, and then up into the blue. For miles and miles and miles they sped along, until they came to the coast of Japan. There Urashima stepped ashore, answered the wistful eyes of the tortoise with a long, lingering gaze of love, and hastened inland.

The tortoise plunged back into the sea, and Urashima was left on the land with a sense of sadness.

He looked about him, recognizing the old landmarks. Then he went up into the village; but, as he went, he noticed with some surprise that everything seemed wonderfully changed. The hills were the same, and, in a way, the village was familiar, but the people who passed him on the road were not those he had known three days ago. Surely three short days would leave him exactly where he stood before he went. Three days could never produce this change. He was at a loss to understand it. People he did not know—strangers in the village, he supposed— passed him by as if he were a complete stranger. Some of them turned and looked at him as one would look at a newcomer. Furthermore, he noticed that the slender trees of three days since were now giant monarchs of the wayside.

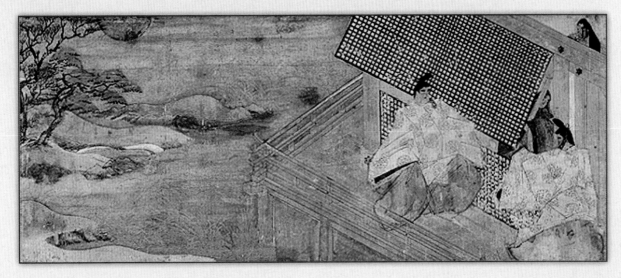

At last, wondering greatly, he came to his old home. How changed it was! And, when he turned the handle of the door and walked in, crying out, "Ho, mother! Ho, father! I have come back at last!" he was met by a strange man barring the doorway.

"What do you want?"

"What do you mean?"

"I live here."

"Where are my father and mother? They are expecting me."

"I do not understand. What is your name?"

"Urashima Taro."

"Urashima Taro!" cried the man in surprise.

"Yes, that is my name: Urashima Taro!"

The man laughed, as if he saw the joke.

"You don't mean the original Urashima Taro?" he said. "But still, you may be some descendant of him?"

"I do not understand you. My name is Urashima Taro. There is no other who bears that name. I am the fisherman: surely you know me."

The man looked at Urashima very closely to see if he was joking or not.

"There was an Urashima Taro, a famous fisherman of three hundred years ago, but you — you are joking."

"Nay, nay, I am not joking. It is you that are joking with your three hundred years. I left here three or four days ago, and now I have returned. Where have my father and mother gone?"

The man stared at him aghast.

"Are you mad?" he cried. "I have lived in this house for thirty years at least, and, as for your father and mother why, if you are really Urashima Taro, they have been dead three hundred years; and that is absurd. Do you want me to believe you are a ghost?"

"Not so; look at my feet." And Urashima put out one foot and then the other, in full accordance with the Japanese belief that ghosts have no feet.

"Well, well," said the man, "you can't be Urashima Taro, whatever you say, for he lived three hundred years ago, and you are not yet thirty."

With this the man slammed the door in Urashima's face.

What could it all mean? Urashima Taro dead. Lived three hundred years ago. What nonsense! He must be dreaming. He pinched his ear and assured himself that he was not only alive, but wide awake.

Perplexed beyond measure, Urashima resolved to go to the fountain-head and settle the matter once and for all. Turning away, he made all haste to the village. Was this the village he had known? Urashima inquired of a countryman he had never seen before, where the village chronicles were kept.

"Yonder," said the man, pointing to a building which had certainly taken more than three days to erect.

Urashima thanked him and then hastened to the building and went in. He was not long in finding what he wanted. It was an ancient entry, and it ran:

"Urashima Taro — a famous fisherman who lived in the early part of the fourteenth century, the traditional patron demi-god of fishermen. There are many stories concerning this half-mythical character, chief of which is that he hooked a whale far from shore, and, as he would not relinquish the prize, his boat was dragged for ever and ever over the surface of the sea. Mariners of the present day solemnly say that they have seen Urashima Taro sitting in his boat skimming the waves as he held the line by which he had caught the whale. Whatever the real history of

30

Urashima Taro, it is certain that he lived in the village, and the legend concerning him is the subject of great interest to visitors from the great land of America."

Urashima shut the book with a slam and went away, down to the seashore. As he went, he realized that those three days he had spent in perfect happiness with the Princess were not three days at all, but three hundred years. His parents were long since dead, and all was changed. What else could he do but go back to the Dragon kingdom under the sea?

But when he reached the shore, he found no tortoise ready to take him back, and, after waiting a long time, he began to think his case was hopeless. Then, suddenly, he bethought himself of the little box which the Princess had given him. He drew it forth and looked at it. He had promised her not to open it, but what did it matter now?

So he sat down on the seashore, untied the fastenings of the little box and then lifted the lid. He was surprised to find that the box was empty; but, slowly, out of the emptiness came a little thin, purple cloud which curled up and circled about his head. It was fragrant, and reminded him of the sweet perfume of the Princess's robes.

Suddenly he stood up, thinking he heard her sweet voice calling him. For a moment he stood there, a splendid figure of early youth. Then a change came over him. His eyes grew dim, his hair turned silvery white, lines came upon his face, and his form seemed to shrivel with extreme old age.

Then Urashima Taro reeled and staggered to and fro. It only took a moment for Urashima to age from a young and healthy 30 year old, to an ancient and frail, three hundred year old man.

The End